Adventures of the Animal Town Aviators

Good Will Trip Around the World

Book I

Written and Illustrated by H. Boylston Dummer

Books from

THE CHRISTIAN SCIENCE MONITOR.

Boston, Massachusetts

Adventures of the Animal Town Aviators- Book I
Written and illustrated by H. Boylston Dummer.

Compiler and editorial director, Claire M. Stoddard of
Stoddard Productions, New York.
Designed and typeset in Goudy by Polese Clancy, Boston.
Illustrations adapted for color by Ellen Crouch.
Editorial assistance by Editorial Services of New England, Inc.,
Cambridge, Massachusetts.
Printed and bound in the U.S.A. by Worzalla,
Stevens Point, Wisconsin.

ISBN 0-87510-198-4

Travelog

This is a book of promise...of peace...of fulfillment. It is also a delightful book about a courageous group of animal adventurers who set off on an incredible around-the-world trip.

The Animal Town stories, written and illustrated by H. Boylston Dummer, appeared in the Christian Science Monitor in 1936 and 1937. Mr. Dummer was a New Englander, born in Byfield, Massachusetts. A well-known landscape artist, he specialized in oils, but was skillful in watercolors and etchings as well. Mr. Dummer's love for nature and for the animals that live in the natural world led him to thoughts of bringing some of his animal friends to life for children and, thus, Animal Town was born.

In these stories, the animals promise to spread good will to all they meet. This promise is fulfilled with a spirit of peace and harmony established wherever they travel.

Today the world hungers for the fulfillment of this same promise. Hope for world calm depends on young people who, with their childlike trust, extend their goodwill to others.

Animal Town folk excited over round-the-world flight

Grampa Bear almost wishes he were going along.

Animal Town Prepares for Take-Off

"**S**ay, Reddy! Reddy! Just a minute!" Reddy Fox was hurrying across Animal Town Square when he was hailed by Grampa Bear:

"What's all this excitement—fire, or a parade, or something?"

"No," said Reddy, "haven't you heard the big news, Grampa Bear?"

"No, I can't say that I've heard any special news that would cause all you Animal Town folks to act as if you'd lost your heads. Of all the hurrying and scurrying! I thought something must be up."

"Well, we hope it will be 'up' tomorrow," chuckled Reddy.

"What will be up?" asked Grampa.

"Why, the airplane we animals are building. And when it is finished, five of us—Buster Bear, Bunny Rabbit, Racky Coon, Reddy Squirrel, and I—are going out West to visit some of our relatives in Yellowstone Park, and maybe to Alaska, or even round the world!"

"Well, well!" chuckled Grampa Bear. "What an idea! But how do you know that machine of yours will fly?" he asked.

"We don't," replied Reddy, "but we think it will, and that's a big start, you know. Well, I must be going; they sent me after this pot of glue," and away he started. But he had had his head turned talking to Grampa and not watching where he was going, and so he stubbed his toe on an upturned root, which sent him sprawling—and spilled the glue all over himself!

The animals came rushing up. "Anything the matter, Reddy?" they chorused.

"No," answered Reddy pluckily, "I'm just stuck on my job, that's all!"

"Well," said one of the animals, "it's nothing serious if he can spring an old joke like that."

"We must have more cloth for the wings, "said Racky Coon.

Grampa Bear had ambled up to the working group, and called out,"Say, Racky, I have two big sheets you may have, and they are good and stout."

He hurried off to his cabin to get the sheets. In almost no time he was back with the cloth which was enough to finish the wings of the airplane.

Grampa Bear was more than interested; in fact, he was getting about as excited as anyone.

"What are you going to use for a motor?" he asked his nephew, Buster Bear.

"Oh," said Buster, "that's all taken care of. We found an old automobile left in the woods and we have taken out the engine. Tomorrow we are going to try it out in our plane!"

"My, my!" grunted Grampa. "If I wasn't so busy, I'd like to take the trip myself. I have a cousin out there in the West, Silvertip Grizzly Bear. He told me once when he paid us a visit years ago that Yellowstone Park was a wonderful place. No one is allowed to have a gun in the park, so the animals don't have to worry about hunters. As I remember it, he told about some hot springs, where you could put your food and in a few minutes it would be cooked. Doesn't seem possible, but that's what he told us."

How the airplane grew, with all the busy animals working on it! Some were looking the engine over, others were painting the body of the plane. So the daylight hours slipped away and the animals one by one returned to their homes tired but happy.

When the moon came up over the hill in back of Animal Town, all the animals were asleep dreaming of the morrow when the homemade machine would be given its trial flight—that is, if it would fly.

Animal Town Aviators take off on round-the-world flight

"She's leaving the ground!" yelled Grampa Bear.

The Home-made Plane Heads Westward

nimal Town was wide awake, though it was still dark. This was to be the biggest day in the history of this wilderness town, the day when the new airplane would be tried out, and perhaps the Animal Town Aviators' good will trip round the world would start!

Grampa Bear, blinking in the early light, nearly bumped into his nephew, Buster Bear, who was hurrying to the plane with a roll of blankets.

"Good morning, Grampa! I didn't suppose you would be up for a couple of hours yet," said Buster.

"Well, I couldn't sleep much, and I just lay there wondering about this plane of yours. You have it built, and the engine installed, and yet I haven't heard anything about gas. What are you going to use for gas?"

"Now Grampa," answered Buster Bear, "don't let that bother you. You know, foxes are pretty smart. Reddy Fox's daddy is just about as smart as they come, and he has invented a gas that will give much more power than any other gas now made. And the wonderful part of it is that it can be made as you need it!"

The Mayor was standing on the plane, making a little speech in honor of the animals who were starting their trip around the world. He praised them for their courage and spoke of all the stories they would be able to bring back to Animal Town. Then he said, "I have here something that I'm sure will prove very useful on your trip," and he held up a large compass. "This has been the property of the town for many years, and we have never had any use for it. Now I present it to you, Reddy Fox, as the leader of our Animal Aviators. May it keep you on a straight course, and help you return to us safely! We are proud of you and will await with great interest your return."

The world voyagers tried to appear as if they were not affected by all this praise; that is, all except Buster Bear. His chest kept swelling larger and larger. Doc Coon said, "If the Mayor doesn't stop praising Buster he'll surely bust—or something."

Just then there was a great commotion on the outskirts of the crowd, and a shrill voice said, "Don't go till I get there! Hold everything!" The animals

stretched their necks to see who was coming. Someone was pushing through the crowd. It was Granny Coon. She was waving something in her hand. "Here is something I've just finished for you animals!" she said. And she held up a fine banner with the words on it: **Animal Town Aviators' Good Will Trip Around The World.**

Then a new sound was heard. Suddenly the animals realized that it came from the engine of the plane, which was really running! Then, as it grew louder, they set up a great shout. The airplane seemed to tremble for a moment. Then it started slowly across Animal Town Square. Faster and faster it went.

Grampa Bear yelled, "She's leaving the ground! Oh, Boy! She is! She is!"

Such yells and cheers! Never before in its history had there been so much excitement in Animal Town.

Many of the baby animals were held aloft on their parents' shoulders to watch the departure of the good will plane, which had just skimmed over the town hall. The Animal Aviators were waving their last 'good-bys.' So, with banner waving, the plane was headed westward to grand experiences and exciting adventures.

O, they sail through the air with almost the greatest of ease

ANIMAL TOWN AVIATORS

GOOD WILL TRIP AROUND THE WORLD

With so much rushing from side to side, Buster Bear
finds the plane a bit difficult to steer.

No Sooner Up Than They Get Hungry

loft at last, our Animal Town Aviators went speeding through the sunlight, watching, star-eyed, the ever-changing landscape, so far below.

At first the animals rushed from side to side, as some point of special interest came into view. But Buster called out, "You fellows will have to stop that! You may tip over this plane; and it makes it all the harder to steer!"

On one of the lakes, they saw a large bird with black head and bill, a white collar, and a body spotted with black and white. The bird sent up a weird, cackling call. The animals shouted out, "Say, you bird, are you laughing at our plane? We'll just come down and catch you. This plane can fly faster than you can."

The animals came close to the strange bird. But when they were almost upon him, the bird dived into the water. They circled around waiting for him to come to the surface. As they were waiting, Racky Coon said, "Hm-m, maybe he went down too deep, or maybe he was a fish, or..."

But just then, sharp-eyed Reddy Fox looked out and saw the strange bird come to the surface with a great splatter. The bird stood almost straight up in the water, flapped his wings, and repeated his weird laugh. The animals looked where Reddy pointed. Buster said: "Say! That bird is too much for us. We'll just have to wave him 'good-by' and be on our way. By the way, I have just thought who this bird is. He is the Great Northern Diver, or Loon, the greatest diver in the world! He will come up with just the tip of his bill out of the water, take a breath, and dive again without being seen."

So the plane was headed up over the trees surrounding the lake, and on to the west. By some of the ponds over which the plane flew, the animals saw deer coming down to drink. These beautiful creatures looked up with wonder in their eyes. How strange it was to see animals, that should be on the ground, sailing over their heads, seemingly riding on the back of some strange bird!

As they became hungry, each animal looked into some box or bag and drew out what he wanted to eat. Reddy Squirrel discovered a bag of nuts; and there he stayed, having the time of his life, until Reddy Fox, the leader

of the Animal Aviators, caught him. "Say, you squirrel, you can't eat up all your food so soon. We may not always be able to find food wherever we stop."

"Oh," answered Reddy Squirrel. "I do not wish to stop eating nuts; at least, nut now—I mean not now."

"Well," said Reddy Fox, "I'm boss of this expedition. So you just go easy with those 'nots' and 'nuts.' And you, too, Bunny Rabbit," whom he discovered with a small cabbage, making its green leaves disappear rapidly, crinkling his nose in great enjoyment. "My goodness," added Reddy Fox, "you animals should give your stomachs a rest. You think more about eating than about the wonderful scenery we are passing over. How about you, Racky Coon, what are you doing?"

"I'm not doing anything. Honest, Reddy, I'm not," replied Racky. "But I can't help thinking how good an ear of corn would taste."

"You animals are doing so much talking about eating, you have me thinking about it, too," said Reddy.

"Me, too," announced Buster Bear.

"Guess we'll be landing before long and 'boil kettle,' as the woodsmen of the North say. I'll be on the lookout for a place where we can land."

Mr. Paddletail tells the Aviators how the beavers live

The visitors from Animal Town respectfully decline
an underwater trip to the beaver lodge.

Welcomed to Beaver Village

ook!" shouted Reddy. "Just ahead there seems to be a fine meadow where we can make a landing. There's a pond, too, but there's something odd about this pond. Look at that dam that holds the water back. And what are those queer-looking piles of sticks out there in the water? And someone has been cutting down a lot of trees all along the farther side of the pond."

"Oh, I know," said Buster Bear, "it's a beaver village. I've heard my father tell about them. He thinks they are the smartest animals there are. Oh, Boy! Won't it be fun to visit this village!" And in the excitement and anticipation of visiting a beaver village, the animals forgot all about being hungry.

They circled once or twice over the meadow to see if there were any logs hidden in the grass. Then they made a perfect landing.

"Well, if this is a beaver village, it must be a deserted one," said Racky Coon.

"Oh, no, it isn't," said Buster. "See those white pieces of wood floating in the pond? That means there are beavers here, for those white sticks are poplar wood with the bark eaten off. This is what the beavers live on—poplar bark—and the reason you don't see any beavers is that they work mostly at night. But it won't be long now until night."

"What is that thing out in the pond?" asked Reddy Squirrel from a small stump where he had climbed to get a better view, since he is one of the smallest of the Animal Aviators.

"Yes, that's one now! See his black head and those V-shaped ripples. He's swimming," said Buster Bear. "Just wait till he sees us; then watch what he does."

The beaver spied them at that moment. He raised his head and broad tail out of the water, doubling the tail up like a jackknife and bringing it down on the water so that it made a loud sound—a warning.

The black head came up again, and Buster called out, "Mr. Beaver! Mr. Beaver! We're friends from Animal Town."

The beaver did not again slap his tail nor dive, but came swimming straight to the side of the pond where our animal friends were standing. In a few moments he walked ashore with the water dropping from his overalls. He greeted the animals with the words, "Welcome, strangers, to Beaver Village!" Other beavers came swimming up and soon the animals were surrounded by a crowd of curious but good-natured and friendly beavers.

The Animal Towners told the big beaver, who seemed to be the leader, all about their trip around the world, visiting animals of distant lands.

"Well! Well!" said Mr. Paddletail Beaver, "I certainly am interested in your trip; that is, to hear about it. But we beavers don't travel very far. You see, when we eat all the poplar wood in one place, we have to move on, first finding a place where there is plenty of poplar wood, and then building a dam."

The animals began to ask him all sorts of questions, like why and how they built dams.

"Well," said Mr. Paddletail, "when we first came here there was no pond—just a shallow stream. Then we built this dam to hold the water back. Those mounds you see out there in the pond are our lodges, or homes. We have an entrance under water. During the summer, we cut down poplar trees and chop the branches into small enough pieces to handle easily. We then sink them to the bottom of the pond. We must have enough to last us from the time the pond freezes until the ice melts in the spring. So you see

that when the pond is covered with a thick sheet of ice, we are just as

snug as a bug in a rug.

"When we are hungry, all we have to do is to dive down into the water,

take a piece of poplar wood from the bottom of the pond, carry it back up

into the lodge chamber, which is above the water

line, eat the bark off—and it is very good; you'll love

it—then put the sticks back in the pond. When

spring comes, we repair our dam or lodges with

these old sticks.

"Well, I've talked long enough. You animals must

be hungry. Would you like to come down into the lodge

for supper, or would you rather eat here on shore?"

"Mr. Paddletail, we don't wish to hurt your

feelings. You seem so friendly. But if we must dive

down into the pond and come up into your home through that underwater stairway entrance, or whatever you call it, I'm sure we animals would rather eat here on shore. You see, we all had a good bath before we started our good will trip."

Bunny Rabbit easily captures the foot race staged to entertain the beavers

Reddy Squirrel was hoping the race would
be through the tree tops.

Field Day at Beaver Village

As the Animal Aviators sat before their campfire, eating a supper taken from their airplane stores, they saw the moon come up from behind the ridge back of Beaver Town Pond. As it rose higher, the pond was flooded with almost daylight brightness, and the spruces on the opposite shore were brought into silhouette.

Before the moon poured light upon the pond, all nature seemed sleeping. Now, in the brilliant moonlight, the pond became all astir with life.

This was really daytime for Beaver Town, and everyone was busy. Wedge-shaped ripples crossed and recrossed the pond. The young beavers seemed more intent on play, but the older beavers were all active in improving and repairing the dam that made their precious pond possible. Mr. Broadtail Beaver stood on the dam directing the other workers of the village and telling them just what to do.

From the dark spruces came the voice of Mr. Horned Owl. He also awakes whenever night begins.

As Buster Bear sat before the campfire, looking out over this beautiful and peaceful scene, he turned to the other animals and said, "Animals, I wish I were an artist with the ability to put on canvas scenes such as this before us. But wonderful as art is, sleep seems more important, after our long day. Tomorrow we shall take to the air again, and leave this village where we have enjoyed our beaver friends so much. So, animals, let's turn in!"

The other animals needed no urging and in a few minutes they were asleep, resting comfortably on their beds of balsam fir.

It seemed only a few minutes before the sun, sending its warm rays stealing into the camp, awoke them to a new day which promised great

activities. They were still rubbing their eyes sleepily when Mr. Paddletail Beaver appeared, calling out cheerily, "Good morning, friends! I have news that I hope will please you.

"We beavers have prepared a breakfast in your honor—and it won't be all poplar wood." (He added the last remark as he noticed the somewhat doubtful looks on our Animal Aviators' faces.) "I got Mrs. Gray Fox, Uncle Bruin Bear, and others who know what you animals like, to prepare the breakfast; so follow me!"

The Animal Aviators followed Mr. Paddletail to a beautiful little grove, where a fine breakfast was laid out. The animals were shown their places, and then each one was surprised and pleased to find before him just the kind of food he liked best. The beavers meanwhile confined themselves to their poplar wood.

What a breakfast! And how everyone enjoyed it! When the animals had eaten what they wished, Mr. Paddletail made a fine speech. He said that

Beaver Village was very much honored in having a visit from the Animal

Aviators; and he highly praised their idea of visiting all parts of the world on

a good will tour to create a more friendly spirit among all animals.

Then, after Reddy Fox had thanked Mr. Paddletail on behalf of his

friends and himself, they went on a tour of Beaver

Village. They were shown how trees were cut down,

how dams and houses were constructed, and how the

canals were dug out so that, after the nearer trees had

been cut down, trees farther away could be floated

easily out into the pond.

The beavers put on a marvelous exhibition of fancy

diving, which brought cheers from our animal friends.

In their turn, the Animal Aviators put on a foot race

entered into by all except Reddy Squirrel, who said he did not have a chance

unless they raced through the treetops, which he himself just loved to do.

How the animals went through the grass by the edge of the pond! The beavers were amazed at the speed of the animals, for beavers—while they are great workers and very clever—are not built for speed. Mr. Broadtail said he never supposed any animal could go as fast as Bunny Rabbit, who came in first.

Reddy Fox praised Bunny Rabbit and said, "You ran a fine race, but if the race were longer, I think I could beat you."

"So could I," said Buster Bear.

"Me, too!" declared Racky Coon.

"Well, well," said Bunny Rabbit. "You animals seem to be a bit doubtful about my winning. I think you're a little afraid I could win again. Let's have another race, now that you fellows are just getting limbered up."

"No! No!" said Reddy Fox. "I think we have raced enough— anyway, we shall have to say 'good-by' to our beaver friends and take to the air." So saying, he examined the gas supply, for their next hop would be a long one.

With all the animals helping, everything was soon ready. They climbed in, Buster taking the wheel.

"Contact!" yelled Buster.

A helpful beaver gave the propeller a spin, and then took a running dive into the pond.

With a roar, the airplane taxied over the meadow. Then, mounting quickly, it skimmed over the spruces and headed westward. The Animal Aviators waved to their waving beaver friends, who rapidly became just dots so far below.

Once in the air, the Animal Aviators charted a course for their next stop, Yellowstone Park.

Animals pilot their plane to Mr. Silvertip's campfire

The big bear's winter sleep wasn't finished, so the aviators had to awaken their host.

Aviators Arrive at Yellow-stone

ll day Buster Bear kept the good will plane roaring through the air. The animals watched lakes and forests as they slipped quickly past beneath them. In the distance could be seen a range of mountains with their tops covered with snow. "Let's go up nearer to the snow line," said Racky Coon. "But it surely is getting colder." The aviators looked over their luggage and brought out warm clothes, which they had not expected to use until they had gone a long way farther north. The animals could not understand how it could be so cold, when it had been so warm in the valley.

Soon they were quite close to the mountains. They decided to get a good look at the snow-capped ranges before going down to make camp. Their camping spot was to be in a large grove of trees that seemed like toy trees from the great height at which the airplane was sailing.

Racky Coon said that he liked scenery, but if he could only get a near view of a campfire, he would be better satisfied.

"Well," said Reddy Fox, "I think that I could stand the sight of a nice fire, too, so we'll start looking for one, Racky." As he said this, the air grew colder and snow began to fall. Then a sudden snowstorm almost blotted out the landscape.

Sharp-eyed Reddy Fox saw a campfire just ahead, almost on top of one of the mountains. Another swirl of snow and the valley and mountains were lost to sight. After dodging stunted trees and huge rocks, the aviators made a landing. Jumping out of the plane, they saw that the fire was in front of a cave and that a big bear was dozing inside.

"Hello!" shouted Reddy Fox, "Hello! Hello!"

Still the big bear dozed on. If he heard Reddy's shouts, they may have seemed

to him like some louder gusts of wind howling past.

"Well," said Buster, "I'm not going to stay here and freeze. Follow me, you animals."

After hurriedly covering the cockpit of the plane, the animals started after Buster. While he had a lot of courage, at the same time he saw to it that he was not very far ahead of the others as he entered the cave. It was nice and warm inside, and it looked interesting. The cave contained a rough table, two chairs, several stools, and two large bunks.

The animals were looking the cave over when they heard a loud, rough grunt, and then a "Whoof! Whoof!" Turning, they saw the big bear partly awake, looking at them sleepily.

Reddy Fox stepped toward the big bear. "How do you do, Mr. Bear?" he said politely. "We are Animal Town Aviators on a good will trip round the world."

Mr. Bear had a struggle getting awake. "Howdy, you animals! Where did you say you were from?"

"Animal Town," said Reddy.

"Animal Town," repeated the big bear. "I was there once."

"Then you must be Mr. Grizzly Silvertip; and this must be Yellowstone Park," said Buster Bear. "My grandfather knows you."

"To be sure, to be sure," said Mr. Silvertip. "Yes, this is Yellowstone Park. I remember your grandfather well. You animals will excuse me if I seem somewhat dull, I'm just waking up from my winter's sleep. I woke up this morning, built a fire, and then went to sleep in my chair. How did you say you got way up here?"

"With our airplane. We built it ourselves," chorused the animals.

"Do tell! Do tell!" exclaimed Mr. Silvertip in astonishment.

"Why did you come way up here, almost to the timber line?" asked Racky

Coon. "I should think you could hunt around down in the valley and find a

place that would be easier to reach. We never should

have found you here if the sudden snowstorm had not

forced us to land. Your campfire helped us greatly."

"Well, you young animals, I'll tell you why I came

up here, if I can keep awake long enough," agreed Mr.

Silvertip. "Years ago, before this region was a park,

we Grizzlies came up here to get away from the hunters.

You know when we Grizzlies sleep, we sleep! Nothing,

hardly, can awaken us. But while we sleep, we snore

like a thunderstorm. The hunters used to tramp all over the mountains looking

for caves and listening for a snoring bear. So all the Grizzlies got into the

habit of coming way up here for their winter's sleep. Even though this is now

a park, in which hunting with guns is forbidden, we come back each autumn

to this spot—just habit, I guess."

Mr. Bear was yawning about every other word. "You animals must be tired.

(Yawn.) You are little fellers. (Yawn.) You can all pile into that other bed. You'll find plenty of blankets." (Yawn, yawn.)

"Thank you, Mr. Silvertip," said Reddy Fox. (Yawn, yawn.) "Now you have me doing it! It's very kind of you (yawn) to let us stay here, even though it has stopped snowing."

"Yes," replied Mr. Silvertip, "it was just a spring squall, but pretty fierce while it lasted. Scurry into that bunk, youngsters. You can pack yourselves in somehow. I'd let one of you sleep with me, but I'm pretty big—almost 1000 pounds—and if I should roll over on you, you would look like an animal cracker—perhaps not so thick." At this last sleepy observation, Mr. Silvertip chuckled quietly. "Now, goodnight, youngsters. Tomorrow I'll be more wide-awake and will show you around the park."

So the Animal Aviators crawled into the bunk, and soon they were all snuggled under warm blankets. For a few minutes they watched the flickering campfire light on the roof of the cave. Then sleepy eyes closed and the only sound heard was the deep breathing of Mr. Silvertip, which no doubt would soon develop into deep snores.

Mr. Bison gives the Animal Town Aviators something to think about

Mr. Silvertip, however, wouldn't let
Mr. Bison buffalo them.

Breakfast and a Bison

r. Silvertip awoke with a start. It took him a few moments to straighten out the events of the previous evening. It seemed like a dream to him. But when he looked toward the other bunk he realized that it was no dream, for there were his little Animal Town visitors all sleeping soundly. He dressed quietly, and then started up the fire, which soon began to crackle and snap. Mr. Silvertip looked around for the frying pan, which he had not used since he had gone to sleep in the late fall. When Mr. Silvertip had found the pan, he was almost overcome with the thought of all these animal visitors, for he had nothing for them to eat, and he knew they would be hungry when they awoke. As for himself, he did not care, for, after awakening from his winter's sleep, he usually ate very little for a few days.

As Mr. Silvertip stood holding the old battered frying pan, Reddy Fox awoke and saw him standing there. Reddy called out, "Good morning,

Mr. Silvertip. We won't allow you to use any of your stores to feed us

animals. I'll get right up and bring in something from our plane."

Mr. Bear started to say something, but Reddy said, "No, we wouldn't think

of eating up your food; it means a lot of hard work for you to bring supplies

way up here."

Mr. Silvertip was chuckling to himself. "My! My! Reddy Fox, you are

a very thoughtful young animal. If you feel that way about it, I suppose I'll

have to give in, but it seems hardly right."

Reddy went out to the plane and brought in enough for a fine meal.

Mr. Silvertip took what Reddy handed to him and started to prepare

breakfast, chuckling all the while. "My!" he said to himself. "That was a

close call. They don't know I hadn't anything to eat, and I didn't have to

apologize for not having any. My lucky day, I call it!"

All the Animal Aviators were now up and wide awake. They stood

in front of the cave looking out at the wonderful mountain view of sparkling snow in the early morning light.

"Come and get it!" shouted Mr. Silvertip. And how the animals rushed into the cave and started to make the food disappear!

"This is some breakfast, Mr. Bear," said Buster Bear. "It surely is," chorused Reddy Fox, Bunny Rabbit, Racky Coon and Reddy Squirrel.

Mr. Silvertip was much pleased with this praise. "Now, youngsters, just as soon as we finish breakfast, I'll start down the mountain and meet you in that grove of trees where you planned to camp last night."

"Well, this is too bad, Mr. Silvertip, but I'm really afraid our plane wouldn't be able to carry your great weight, for you weigh more than we do and all of our supplies together. We feel very sorry."

"Oh, don't you worry one little bit," replied Mr. Silvertip. "I'm not fussy about riding in an airplane, anyway. I can scratch down this mountain so quickly you'll be surprised. It will help me to keep awake, but I'm not so sleepy as I was yesterday." Saying

this, Mr. Silvertip put on his coat and started at a great

pace down the trail.

Buster Bear said, "I think Mr. Silvertip is a fine chap.

I don't like to think of all the distance he has to walk,

while we get into our plane and just glide like a bird

down into the valley. For one thing, I think we should

wash up the dishes and not leave them for Mr. Silvertip

when he returns."

So the Animal Aviators started in and almost before you could say,

"Jack Robinson," the dishes were washed and put back on a big shelf.

"We must now find out if our plane will start," said Buster. The animals

jumped into the plane; that is, all except Reddy Fox, who stood ready to give

the propellers a twist.

Buster turned on the switch. "Contact!" he shouted.

Reddy gave the propeller a turn, and jumped quickly into the plane.

He had no idea of having the others sail away and leave him way up on the mountain.

The plane seemed to hesitate a moment, then taxied over the hard-packed snow, and like a bird, shot into the air.

It was a glorious morning. The animals were in high spirits. Here they were, in one of the wonderspots of America—Yellowstone Park. As they sailed down over rocks and trees, they spied Mr. Silvertip making his way with long strides down the mountain. He was much farther down than they expected to find him. Racky said, "He surely is scratching his way down quickly, as he said he could."

Soon they landed in a level spot, covered with green grass and flowers, near the grove of trees where they were to wait for Mr. Silvertip.

Near by were some great shaggy beasts. At the sight of them, Racky started to climb a tree.

"Why, Racky," said Buster Bear, "those are bison—some call

them 'buffaloes.' They wouldn't hurt you."

One, that was larger than the rest, came ambling up, looking over the animals and their plane. "Where did you get that?" he asked sharply, as he pointed his foot to an old fur robe that the animals had brought with them.

"Why, Mr. Bison, that is an old robe we brought from Animal Town," replied Buster.

Mr. Bison began to roar. "That robe, as you call it, is the skin of a bison! There used to be millions of us out here, until the hunters came. Now what have you to say for yourselves?" And he bellowed again.

The little Animal Aviators stood huddled near the plane. But just at this moment, Mr. Silvertip came up. The animals told him what Mr. Bison had said.

Mr. Silvertip turned on him, and he stepped back, for he was no match for Mr. Silvertip, the grizzly bear. "What do you mean by frightening my little friends? Even if that is a bison skin, these animals had nothing to do with it. Did you ever hear of one animal pointing a gun at another? Answer me!"

"No, Mr. Silvertip. I can't say honestly that I ever did. I beg the pardon of all you little animals," and Mr. Bison ambled back to his companions, who were looking on with great interest at these flying animals.

But at that moment, the only things of interest to our Aviators were the wonderful things they were about to see in Yellowstone Park.

Animal Town Aviators inspect Yellowstone's geysers

But the youngsters think that this sort of thing
would keep them in hot water.

Seeing Yellowstone Park

ow Mr. Bison had returned to the herd with a deep, rumbling bellow. As he saw Mr. Silvertip looking in his direction, he stopped his rumbling and started eating the rich park grass.

"Well, Mr. Silvertip," said Reddy Fox, "you didn't let him buffalo you."

"No siree," replied Mr. Silvertip, with a huge grin. "Now, that that's over with, how about seeing something of the Yellowstone Park?"

"Say," spoke up Racky Coon, "I think it would be a good thing to take a little walk around the outside of the park first, then look at the interesting things inside."

"Well," said Mr. Silvertip, "how much time can you spare for this?"

"Why," said Racky, "we could do it in a couple of hours, couldn't we?"

"A couple of hours!" exclaimed Mr. Silvertip, and he started laughing uproariously. The other animals stood by soberly. Then, Mr. Silvertip,

seeing this, stopped laughing and said, "You young animals, please excuse

me, but it struck me funny—your thinking that you could walk around

Yellowstone Park in two hours! Why, youngsters, Yellowstone Park is

much too big to walk around in a couple of hours." He continued:

"Why, we have one lake in the park 20 miles long, with a shore line over

100 miles long, and this in itself would keep you moving to do it in two

hours. And mountains! If you boys are looking for mountains, you need

look no farther. We have 24 peaks in the park, every one over

10,000 feet high!

"Goodness me," concluded Mr. Silvertip, "you animals must be tired of

standing here listening to a lecture on the park. What you need, I'm sure,

is to see some of these wonders. There are hot springs and geysers all over

the park. There is one very fine geyser near here. I'll show it to you."

As Mr. Silvertip ambled off, the Animal Aviators hopped into their

precious plane and followed. When they saw Mr. Silvertip standing still,

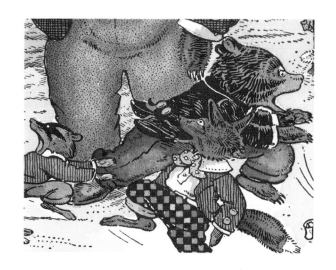

they stopped the plane and joined him. "This," he said, "is Old Faithful, probably the most famous geyser in the park."

The animals all crowded around to see everything possible. As they looked there came a hiss, and a column of water shot more than a 100 feet into the air. How the animals scampered away! But Mr. Silvertip called to them that there was no danger, and explained that this geyser shot a stream of hot water 125 feet into the air every 65 minutes.

All the animals had returned but Reddy Squirrel, so Mr. Silvertip called out, "Don't you wish to look at this wonder of nature?"

"Yes, I do," said Reddy, "but if you don't mind, I'd like to look at some wonders of nature that are not so jumpy. This one would keep me in hot water all the time." The other animals laughed at this, thinking it a pretty clever thing for a little squirrel to say.

Mr. Silvertip then showed them another geyser, called the Giant, which at uncertain times throws a stream of hot water 200 feet into the air and keeps it up for over an hour.

Reddy was still upset and said, "If this geyser is uncertain when it will spout, I am certain that I do not wish to be there when it does!"

The aviators were introduced to many animals—moose, deer, antelope, mountain sheep, and goats, and a great many bears. One big black bear looked over the good will plane and started laughing. When Buster Bear asked him what he was laughing at, he said, "To think that you animals should suppose that you could fly in that thing."

"Well, we'll show you," said Buster. "Hop in, you animals, and we'll show him whether this bird can fly or not."

Reddy Fox was the last one in, when Buster yelled, "Contact!" He gave the propeller a spin and jumped in. The plane soared into the air, but above the roar could be heard Mr. Black Bear shouting, "That piece of junk can never fly."

"Well, what do you suppose he thinks we are doing now?" said Buster Bear.

"I don't know," replied Reddy. "Some animals, as well as humans, just can't be shown."

"Well," said Racky, "if I had to live near him, there would be trouble Bruin. But now we should be moving on. If we stay too long in one place, we'll be as old as Grampa Bear back in Animal Town, before we complete our trip round the world."

They had already said 'good-by' to Mr. Silvertip and thanked him for all his kindness. He had advised them to head out over the Great Falls of the

Yellowstone Park, and gave them directions, saying, "You cannot miss them. But, youngsters, I'll miss you!"

It seemed no time at all before the Great Falls came into sight. All the animals were silent at this work of nature—the river rushing along, tumbling more than 300 feet into the canyon.

As they circled the wonderful falls, Bunny Rabbit said, in a timid voice,
"I guess the shower is over."

"What shower?" the animals chorused. "We've had no shower."

"Well that's what I thought," said Bunny, "until I
saw that rainbow at the foot of the falls—and I thought
rainbows never appeared until a shower was over."

"Well, they tell me," said Reddy Fox, "that when
falls have a rainbow, it is caused by sun showing
through the spray."

"I've seen so many wonderful things on this trip,"
said Bunny. "I shouldn't be surprised at anything from
now on."

"You wouldn't, huh!" said Buster Bear. "I've an idea
we haven't seen anything yet."

So the Aviators checked their charts and plotted a course for the
Canadian Rockies.

Animal Town Aviators meet the Big Horn Sheep and Rocky Mountain Goats

Mrs. Nanny saw to it that the visitors didn't get her goat.

In the Canadian Rockies

Buster Bear and Reddy Fox had taken turns piloting the Animal Town plane through the starlit night. Now the east was taking on a rosy tint, showing the near approach of dawn. Stronger and stronger grew the light until at last the sun rose from behind a great range of massive snow-capped mountains. The Animal Aviators held their breath as the wondrous scene unfolded before them. At last Reddy Fox said: "This doesn't seem real! In the Animal Town library is a book which tells all about the Alps in Switzerland, and they must be magnificent; but they say these Canadian Rockies are dozens of Switzerlands rolled into one. Just look at all the snow-capped mountains! And talk about color! What a place for an artist!"

Before the other animals had anything to say, Racky Coon pointed to something far below. "What is that? Looks like a toy building."

The animals looked, and Reddy Fox said, "That toy building is one of the largest hotels in the Canadian Rockies. I know it by the pictures I've seen. Over there to the left is Lake Louise; and over there is Mt. Assiniboine. We must see all we can. And we shouldn't miss Emerald Lake, Lake McArthur, Consolation Lake, and all the others."

"Isn't there a glacier around here?" asked Racky Coon.

"Yes, there is," said Reddy, "the Yoho Glacier."

As the good will plane circled the mountains, the animals became so excited they rushed from side to side. Buster Bear said, "I think we'd better land and give you animals a chance to chase around these mountains. One thing is, you can't tip them over— but you might this plane! This is a good will trip to visit other animals, and I see down below some Big Horn Sheep and Rocky Mountain Goats."

The other animals thought it would be great sport to visit these animals they had never seen before; so Buster, seeing a fairly smooth ledge, brought the plane down safely, and how the Big Horns and White Goats scrambled out of sight!

The Animal Aviators laughed at this. Reddy Fox shouted, "Say, you! We are friends come to visit you." Then they noticed one old white-whiskered goat peeking around a ledge; then others, until a crowd of Big Horns and White Goats gradually gathered around.

One old Nanny Goat holding a young kid goat by the front foot, would not come very near, nor would she let her play with Racky Coon when he tried to. "Say, you strange animal," said Mrs. Nanny, "are you trying to get my goat?"

The other animals let out a shout of laughter at this.

Soon all were having a fine time asking questions and being shown the sights. Near them was a very deep canyon; the walls were about thirty feet apart and almost smooth. Reddy Fox tried looking down but said it made him skittish.

"That's nothing," said a young, strong Big Horn sheep, "I go down there quite often."

"Go down there?" said Reddy Fox. "You'd get a good tumble."

"Is that so?" said the Big Horn. "I'll show you." And he rushed to the edge and leaped off toward the other side.

The Animal Aviators went as near the edge as they dared, expecting to see him go kerflop; but nothing like this happened. The Big Horn landed many feet below on the opposite side, just for an instant, then back on the other side. Back and forth he went, dropping many feet at each jump, until they saw him land safely far below.

"That's what all of us sheep and goats do," said Mr. Billy Goat.

"On these seemingly smooth walls are places just rough enough to get a foot hold to spring back to the other side. That's the way we escape from the hunters."

The Animal Aviators thanked their new friends for all their kindness, and then jumped into their good will plane to continue their sight-seeing tour.

Animal Town Aviators enjoy the Canadian sulphur springs

Buster Bear would have stayed all day but Reddy Fox
convinced him to come back to the airplane.

First a Swim, Then a Zoo Visit

What a grand time the Animal Aviators had, guiding their good will plane around the Canadian rockies! As they circled out over Lake Louise, on one side of the lake the snowy peaks were bathed in golden sunlight. The other shore was vivid with flowers, flaming poppies, deep tinted violets, anemones, columbine, and others. In the background was a tall spruce forest; and in back of the peaks was the glittering Victoria glacier.

They brought the plane down for a few minutes, in order to study and enjoy the scenery.

Mr. Big Horn Sheep had told the Animal Aviators about the warm sulphur springs; so Racky Coon said, "We might as well hunt up these springs." So all the animals jumped into the plane.

They were soon in the air again, but not for long, for they spied the large spring which fit the description given them by their Big Horn friend.

Quickly the animals got into their swim suits, and what a time they had, especially Buster Bear! He would have stayed in all day if Reddy Fox had not said, "If you don't come out I'll take the other animals in the plane and leave you here."

The animals quickly dressed and jumped into the plane again. As they sailed along, they looked down and saw a lot of cages with animals in them.

"Is that a jail? And have those animals done something wrong?" asked Racky Coon.

"No," said Reddy Fox, the wise one of the party, "they are captured and placed in the cages and called a zoo, so human beings can see and study them."

"Well," said Buster Bear, "what a terrible life, with just a few feet of a small enclosure to live in—while we can go where we wish."

"Well," said Reddy Fox, "I see no men around; let us land near and visit this zoological park."

"Suppose we get captured and have to stay here— then no around-the-world trip!" said Racky.

Bunny Rabbit and Reddy Squirrel said they would feel better to stay in the plane.

With a grand sweep, Buster brought the plane safely to the ground. Buster Bear, Reddy Fox, and Racky Coon got out of the plane and approached the cages timidly. They looked everywhere for signs of a man. As they approached the cages, they saw in one a big brown bear larger than they had ever dreamed a bear could be.

Racky Coon said, "There is no such animal as that; you can't fool me."

"Well," said Buster Bear, "don't you see him moving around?"

Just then the big bear showed a little interest. "What's the big idea of riding around in an airplane?"

"We are animals from Animal Town," Said Buster. "We built our airplane and are on a good will trip, visiting animals all over the world. Our next stop will be Alaska."

"Alaska! Did you say Alaska?" And he jumped against the cage with such force that the Animal Aviators thought he would break out. Then he quieted down and asked the animals to pardon him.

"Why are you in here?" asked Buster. "Did you do something wrong?"

"No, never," said Mr. Brown Bear. "I used to live happily up in Alaska with my mate, Mrs. Kodiak Bear, and our little cubs. One day Mrs. Bear asked me to go down to the animal store, some little distance from our home, and on the way back a lot of men captured me and brought me here, and I've been here a long time. Now, this is bad enough, but the worst thing is that Mrs. Bear perhaps thinks I ran away. Say, if you good will animals wish to do a good turn, I wish you would

explain to my wife what happened."

Just then Mr. Bear let out a great roar. "Run, you animals, run, a man is coming!"

The Animal Aviators rushed wildly to their plane—and roared into the air. "My!" said Reddy Fox, "That was a close call! I feel all prickly now."

The keeper had rushed up, wondering about the commotion, as it was before the time the park was opened up to visitors. But when he saw the dressed-up animals jump into an airplane, he stopped and rubbed his eyes.

Just then Mr. Brown Bear let out a funny-sounding grunt. The keeper turned suddenly and said, "Things are getting worse by the minute. Sounds as if that Big Brown Bear was laughing at me." But as he went up to the cage, Mr. Bear was just nosing around his feed dish, and then jumped into his pool with a great splash that sent a shower of water all over the bewildered keeper!

The park was now just a speck in the distance, and the Animal Aviators were quieting down. "Where are we headed for now, may I ask?" said Bunny Rabbit.

"Yes, you may ask," said Reddy Fox, "and the best part is I can answer. Our next stop is Alaska, the land of great caribou herds, lofty mountains, and the great river Yukon—the river of the golden sands!"

Animal Town Aviators try their paws at panning gold in Alaska

Mr. Miner Bear shows the youngsters how to wash pay dirt.

In Alaska, the Land of Gold

uster Bear was heading the good will plane almost due north, and all was well. Reddy Fox had brought along a geography book from the Animal Town School and told the Animal Aviators about the points of interest they were sailing over. One place nestled among the mountains they felt must be Wrangell.

Reddy Fox said, "While this is a good will trip, visiting animals all over the world, I think we should learn something of the country we pass over. We shall soon pass over the old Treadwell Gold Mine at Douglas Island, said to have been one of the greatest gold mines in the world, until a great blast blew out the top of the mine and let in water. Think of all the gold taken out of Alaska!"

"How long since have they taken any gold out of Alaska?" asked Racky Coon.

"Well," said Reddy Fox, "they have never stopped taking it out. Over the years, millions of dollars worth of gold have been taken out."

"I wish we could find some gold," said Racky, "so we could take it back to Animal Town and build a new library with a museum attached so we could display the specimens we collect all over the world."

"That's a great idea!" chorused the other animals. "I think we may be able to do it, at that."

They headed the plane up over the Chilkoot and White Horse Pass, where during the gold rush of 1897 and 1898 an almost continuous line of miners struggled though the snow.

The plane was now headed almost due west. "There isn't anything but mountains and streams up here," said Buster. "Some seem to be pretty high, much higher than we are sailing."

"Yes," said Reddy Fox, "we are going to pass near Mt. McKinley, the highest mountain on the North American Continent, 20,300 feet high."

Soon this great mountain began to loom up above the other mountains;

and when the aviators came near enough to get a good view of it, they again headed north for the great Yukon, almost 2400 miles long, the river of the golden sands.

The animals were looking with sharp eyes on the ground below, as Buster was flying the plane lower all the time. Finally, they came to a small stream flowing into the Yukon, and Reddy Fox spied a rough cabin on the bank.

"Look!" said Reddy, "there is a bear with a big pan standing in the stream. Oh! I know what he is doing. He's washing gold. Let's go down and perhaps he will show us how."

So the plane was brought down near the camp, and the animals jumped out and shouted to the big bear. His eyes were almost popping out of his head, his lower jaw dropped, then he let out a whole string of "whoops," dropped his pan, which went clattering onto the rocks in the stream, and started like a streak for the cabin. He dashed into it and slammed the door, and they heard a

bolt slip into place.

"Well," said Racky, "he certainly seems glad to see us!"

How the animals shouted with glee. Then they saw

the big bear peeking out of the window, but his expres-

sion had changed; and soon they heard the bolt sliding

back. The door opened, and out he came, looking

somewhat silly.

"Well, you young strangers did throw a panic into this old miner. What is

that thing you are riding in?"

"That's an airplane," said Reddy Fox.

"Never saw one before," said Mr. Miner Bear. "What's the big idea? I'm

awfully green on what's going on in the world."

So Reddy Fox told him all about their trip.

"Do tell!" said Mr. Miner Bear. "This sounds interesting. And the

strange thing about that bear you saw in the zoo, we know all about him.

He used to live just a few miles from here. Mrs. Bear, his wife, still lives in the old cabin with their cubs, which are pretty big bears now. I will be sure to see her for you and deliver her husband's message."

The Animal Aviators soon made themselves at home. After they had had a bite to eat, the animals gathered around to hear Mr. Miner Bear tell stories about big gold strikes.

"The big gold rushes are over," said Mr. Bear, "but almost every stream contains gold. By steadily washing the sand, you will soon have quite a little gold dust and perhaps a few nuggets."

He then hunted up all the pans he had, so that each animal could have a chance at the gold. Mr. Bear, with his big pan, scooped up about half a panful of sand and water from the stream. Then he began to swirl the pan. This swirling motion allowed the lighter sand and dirt to be washed over the sides of the pan, leaving the heavier pebbles and any gold that might be in the sand at the bottom of the pan.

Mr. Bear had to try several times before any color, or "pay dirt," showed up. But when a few grains of gold did show up at last, the animals let out a great shout. Then each animal waded into the stream with his pan and started in to make a fortune. How the animals did work! They washed, splashed, and slipped, and soon their clothes were soaking wet.

Their success was not startling—just a very few golden grains. Reddy Squirrel was the first one to stop. He looked half drowned as he crawled out and sat on the bank drying his clothes and fur. Bunny Rabbit said, "I guess I am rich enough. A few tender leaves are better than gold, which one can't eat anyway."

Soon Reddy Fox said he guessed he'd call it a day.

Mr. Miner Bear had enjoyed the young animals so much that he felt sorry to think of their leaving. He called the animals together and said, "I've never had so much pleasure in my life as I had since you came. My tastes are simple and I wish to add what gold I've saved up to what you have, so that your new library and museum can be built."

The animals nearly lost their breath at this. Then they swarmed all over him, thanking him. Mr. Miner Bear's eyes were misty as he lifted up the tin

can full of golden sand and nuggets from beneath the cabin floor and placed it in Reddy Fox's paws. Reddy started to say,"You shouldn't do this..."

But Mr. Bear stopped him, saying, "Not another word from you animals. I wish to do this; and the memory of this visit will mean a thousand times

more to me than the gold I'm passing on to you."

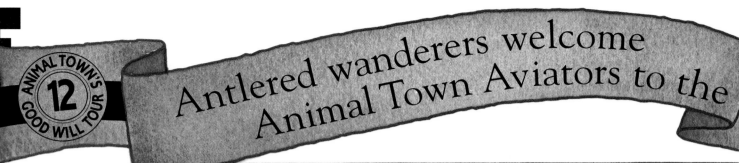

The caribou had seen airplanes before,
but never one piloted by animals!

Aviators Call on the Caribou

lthough the Animal Town Aviators were sorry to leave Mr. Miner Bear, they were excited at the thought that on the morrow they would again be in the air, headed for new sights. So the animals started packing up the plane. When this was finished, the sun had dropped out of sight, and the animals went into Mr. Miner Bear's cabin for the last time. After a pleasant evening, the animals crawled into their comfortable bunks.

The next morning, after a fine breakfast, they said 'good-by' to Mr. Miner Bear and soon the plane was roaring over the mountains again, with the animals looking with bright eyes at the landscape sliding so rapidly behind them.

Racky Coon said, "There must be a great reindeer stable up here. Just look—there are hundreds of them!"

"No," said Reddy Fox, "those are very much like the reindeer, but they are caribou. Probably they are on one of their migrations from one feeding ground to another. They seem always to be on the move."

They watched the caribou swim a river and then go scampering up over a small hill. Reddy Fox said, "We are seeing a more wonderful sight than we realize. Wish we could see them a little closer and talk to them."

"Well," said Buster, "if that's the way you animals feel, we'll glide down."

The other animals thought it would be great sport, so Buster made a landing on the bank of the river that the caribou were swimming across. They kept going past the plane and did not seem to be frightened. "Guess they have seen airplanes before," said Buster.

Just then a big caribou stopped and said: "Greetings, animals. We have seen airplanes before, but never one driven by animals.

How come?" So the Animal Aviators told him all about their trip.

"Well," said Mr. Caribou, "that sounds pretty fine. You say this is a good will trip. Perhaps you can help us. We are moving to find better feeding grounds. Have you seen anything we could eat?"

All the animals said they were very sorry but they had seen nothing that

animals could eat—that is, nothing but great quantities of moss and lichens, just a few miles back.

"What do you mean? 'Nothing but moss and lichens.' That's what we caribou live on. Well, thanks for the good news. I must be going." And he shook his antlers and trotted away to catch up with the swiftly moving herd.

"Well, can you beat that?" said Buster.

"Imagine living on that stuff! I think it is a good idea we don't all like the same kind of food. That was very interesting, but we'll now get this old sky bus to percolating." And in a minute they were in the air again.

"You spoke about reindeer," said Racky to Reddy Fox. "Well, years ago they did bring some reindeer over from Siberia, but I don't know how well they got along."

"Say," said Reddy Squirrel, who was looking intently over the side of the plane, "I've made lots of mistakes, but it seems to me some of those rocks down below are walking around."

What a good time the animals had over this.

"Rocks walking!" shouted Buster Bear. "This is the best yet."

"Well," said Reddy Fox, "there is something, at that, moving down there among the rocks on that hillside. We had better see what it is." So down the plane came again. "You make me stop so often, I might as well drive a milk wagon."

The laugh was stopped when the plane came down near some strange colored birds.

"Well," said Racky Coon, "Reddy Squirrel could be dumber; those birds are colored about like these rocks—white, brown, and black."

"I've been trying to think," said Reddy Fox, "what these birds are, and now I have it. They are Ptarmigans belonging to the grouse family—and Old Mother Nature has sure given them protective coloring. In summer when the ground is bare with brown and white stones, these birds seem to become part of the hillside. Then, when the early snows come, they begin to turn white to match the snow patches; and when Old Man Winter settles down for good, they turn pure white except for two black spots on the outside of the tail."

"I suppose they had to have some way or they would lose track of each other altogether," said Racky.

"Maybe," said Reddy Fox. "Most everything in nature means something; it's not just chance that things are the way they are."

"Well, we can't stay here too long," said Buster. "All right,"chirped

Bunny Rabbit, "pile in and off we go."

As they sailed along, they saw two enormous moose, bigger than they had ever seen before, and one herd of musk ox, shaggy creatures—about the only animals that live so far north that are not white the year round.

The plane began to climb higher, and far, far in the distance could be seen dark blue water; and beyond that the white of snow or ice. On and on the good will plane went, heading north to new adventures.

Animal Town Aviators build a snow North Pole

NORTH POLE

REACHED BY THE ANIMAL TOWN AVIATORS

DUMMER

But they don't know whether to call it
a polar bear or a bear pole!

Aviators Reach the North Pole

Our daring Animal Town Aviators were headed for the North Pole, over glittering ice fields and long stretches of dark blue ocean. Reddy Fox was studying the maps in the old geography book that he had brought. He always kept track of the country they passed over; and at the height that Buster Bear was keeping the plane, the land looked almost like a map.

"Where is the Pole, anyway?" asked Buster Bear. "It wouldn't stick up out of the ocean, would it? Peary found it in 1909, but I don't know what he did with it."

"Has anyone else ever reached the Pole?" asked Racky.

"Yes," said Reddy Fox, "Admiral Byrd reached the Pole and there have been others too!"

"That's nothing!" piped up Reddy Squirrel. "I imagine hundreds of birds have reached the Pole."

"Oh, this was not a real bird I am thinking about. This was a human

Byrd, riding in an airplane like ours," said Reddy Fox.

"A human bird!" exclaimed Reddy Squirrel.

"I should say so," said Reddy Fox.

"Oh just 'say so,'" replied the little squirrel.

He did not like to own up that he did not understand

everything the others did.

The other animals were watching a strange light

that kept streaming up into the sky, and they could

hear a strange crackling sound. "If we could only

store this electric light, we could light Animal

Town," observed Reddy Fox.

"Old Doc Owl wouldn't like that," said Reddy Squirrel.

"What is this strange light?" asked Buster Bear. "It makes me feel

rather creepy."

"Those are the Northern Lights or Aurora Borealis," said Racky Coon.

"What did you say Alice's first name was?" asked Reddy Squirrel.

Buster Bear shook with glee at this. "He's trying to give us one of those 'Knock, Knock' stunts: 'Who's there?' 'Alice.' 'Alice who?' 'Aurora Borealis!'"

The animals whooped and did all kinds of things animals do when something very funny strikes them—that is, all but the poor little squirrel, who seemed ill at ease.

"Now, Reddy," said Reddy Fox, "don't feel sad. We can't all be expected to know everything. I'll have to own up I did not know much about lots

of things until Buster Bear and I started studying up for this trip."

"I wish I had a camera," said Racky Coon, "so that I could take a picture of the Pole, if we find it."

"Well," said Reddy Fox, the wise one, "I always understood there was no pole at all—just an imaginary one."

"Then," said Racky Coon, "if the Pole is only an imaginary one, I could take an imaginary photo of it with an imaginary camera!"

"Yes," spoke up Reddy Squirrel, "and when you get back to Animal Town you could show it to animals with imagination." How the animals whooped at this!

They now came to a great stretch of ice. Was it ice-coated land or just a frozen sea? They did not know, but according to an instrument that Racky had contrived, they had reached the North Pole. So down onto the ice and snow the plane landed.

"Now," said Reddy Fox, "you can see there is no pole here; so in order to get warm by exercising, let us build one."

So they set to work, and soon a large shaft of ice and snow arose. Buster, being the tallest of our animals, made it look something like a bear.

"Why do you make this pole look like a bear?" asked Racky Coon.

"Why," said Buster, "that would make it a Polar Bear, or a Bear Pole— take your choice."

Reddy Fox said, "We should leave some kind of record to show that we arrived here to those who come later." "I have it!" exclaimed Bunny Rabbit. "You know we brought some sticks and twigs in our plane, so we could build a fire and keep warm. I'll bring some of those small twigs and show you what I mean." Soon he was back with them, and with the help of the other animals, they gave notice to the world that the Animal Town Aviators had reached the North Pole.

The animals felt so proud of their arrival at the Pole that they danced around the pole they had erected. Then Reddy Squirrel said, "We forgot one thing. Excuse me a minute." He raced to the plane and came quickly back with a small American Flag which he asked Buster Bear to place in the snow bear's paw.

Animal Town Aviators rescue a cub from a cake of floating ice

The youngsters didn't see anything so
very green about Greenland.

The White Shores of Green- land

s Buster headed the plane toward the southeast from the North Pole, Reddy Fox said he would read a few notes on Greenland, which according to his maps should show up shortly: "The northern part is known as Peary's Land, the northernmost land. Greenland is the largest island in the world outside of the island-continent Australia, and is 1500 miles long and almost 700 miles wide.

"More than three fifths of the entire surface is covered with an ice sheet. The glaciers are constantly moving toward the sea—some at the rate of almost 100 feet a day."

"What a place to start an ice business," said Racky Coon. "One could get rich in no time; it would be all profit."

"Who would buy your ice?" said Buster Bear.

"I never thought about that," confessed Racky.

Ahead, the ice-clad shores of Greenland came into sight. "My," said Bunny Rabbit, "they should have called this Whiteland! What a shore to try to land on! These ice cliffs must be hundreds of feet high."

"I should say so," said Reddy Fox. "My notes say the northern shore is from 1500 to 3000 feet high."

They were quite close to the shore now, and Buster, who had been flying rather low, had to send the plane much higher to get up over the plateau. As they sailed along the eastern shore for hundreds of miles, the air became warmer and they came to where the glaciers were slowly moving into the sea. Every few minutes great cakes would break off and drop with tremendous splashes into the sea. Wherever they looked could be seen floating ice—from small cakes to great icebergs.

"There's a cake of ice out there that looks a bit strange to me," said Reddy Fox.

"Yes, sir! There is something moving on it. Let us head the plane out

there and see what it is."

Soon they were right over the ice cake; and they could see a small polar bear going from one side of the cake of ice to the other. "What shall we do, Reddy Fox?" said Buster. "That little bear is floating out into the ocean!"

"I know what to do," said Reddy Fox. "Back in Animal Town was an old bear that showed me how to throw a lasso, and I became pretty good at it." As he talked, Reddy was coiling a long piece of rope. Then, moving to the edge of the plane, Reddy threw a loop far out. It settled over the shoulders of the young bear and Reddy drew it taught. The other animals grasped the rope and quickly hoisted the young bear up into the plane.

At first the little white bear would not answer any questions, and only shrank back among the bundles and boxes.

"Where did you come from?" the animals kept asking the little white bear; and at last he pointed toward the mainland to the south.

"Well, we'll take a try anyway," said Buster; and he headed

the plane toward the mainland.

As they neared the mainland, the little white bear found his tongue.
"There is my mamma bear now!"

Even Reddy Fox with his sharp eyes could hardly make out anything; but
now they could all see an enormous white bear rushing up and down the
shore. It was not so steep here, and Buster landed the plane safely on the
ice—only it kept sliding on, but soon stopped. When the
animals constructed the plane they had not taken into
consideration the possibility of landing on ice.

As the plane slid to a landing, Mrs. Polar Bear
jumped to safety behind a high ridge of ice. But soon
she was peeking out at them; and when she heard her
little cub calling to her, she came right out.

Mrs. Polar Bear was so thankful to have her little son
back safe with her again, and she thanked our Animal Aviators and
invited them into her crude dwelling made of ice blocks like an igloo.

The animals were much amused to be in a house made of ice, thinking they would freeze if they remained in there long, but they were astonished to find it so warm and comfortable. They told Mrs. Polar Bear all about their good will trip, visiting animals all over the world.

"Well," said Mrs. Polar Bear, "your Reddy Fox would like, I'm sure, to meet his cousins, the Arctic White and Blue Foxes. There are some that live near here. We'll go right over."

The Animal Aviators were more than delighted to meet their relations. On the way back, they visited some arctic hares; and Bunny Rabbit said, "I'm sure proud to be related to such fine-looking animals."

A short distance below the home of Mrs. Polar Bear the ground was bare in large patches; and Mrs. Polar Bear said, "I'll show you something you probably have never seen before—an Eider duck's nest." So the whole crowd followed her, and soon they were among a whole string of nests.

Bunny Rabbit said, as he put his little paw in the nest, "What a soft bed! I'd like to sleep in one as soft as this."

"Well, there it is, help yourself," said Mrs. Bear.

"The baby ducks left the nest weeks ago."

"What is this soft stuff the nest is lined with?" asked Racky Coon.

"Why, that is eiderdown that the mother duck pulls from her breast; it is collected by humans and sold at high prices to stuff pillows and other things. Incidentally, we have about 125 varieties of birds here—in the summer."

As they stood there talking, Reddy Fox said, "What is that pretty little neighbor of yours over there? Looks like Willie Weasel back in Animal Town, only this one is all white except a black tip on his tail, while Willie has brown fur."

"That is Ernest Ermine," said Mrs. White Bear. "I think he does belong to the Weasel family; but up in the Arctic, they stay white all the year. Farther south they are brown in summer and white in winter. Probably if your Animal Town was farther north, Willie Weasel would be white in winter."

With that, our young aviators climbed once more into their sturdy plane, skidded forward along their icy runway, and took to the air, out across the cold North Atlantic.

Aviators fly round and round while studying a great whale

They thought they had seen some queer fountains; but they turned out to be vapor exhaled by the giant mammal.

Visits With Walruses and a Whale

fter leaving the shores of Greenland, the Animal Town Aviators had not long to wait for new adventures. As they sailed along, not a great height above the waves, they spied some black objects on a large ice floe. "What are those things?" asked Racky Coon. "My, but they are large! And look at those great tusks."

"Where?" said Reddy Fox, who was looking over their food supply stores. "Over there," said Racky as he pointed.

Reddy looked and said: "I should say they are large! But I know what they are. They are walruses. By the way, Buster, is that floe large enough to land on?"

"I guess so, Reddy," said Buster. "Here's for a try anyway." And the plane landed on the ice, not far from the big walruses. And did the walruses look up and seem pleased to meet our animal friends? They just roared and went kerplunk into the sea!

As the swirls of water quieted down, Buster said, "Well, I guess the show is all over." But it was not, for as the animals peered into the water, a great black head appeared close to the floe—then another and another, until six heads were bobbing around. Two had tremendous tusks and very long whiskers. Bunny Rabbit said, "He must have to shave those whiskers with an axe!"

Buster Bear called out, "How do you do, Mr. Walrus?"

"Not so badly, you strange bear. But you did give us quite a start!"

"Well," said Racky, "why don't you come back up on the ice?"

"Not a bad idea," said Mr. Walrus. Soon the ice floe rocked and shook as the great beasts climbed back on the ice. Two were much smaller than the rest, and the older

walrus called them babies.

"Quite sizable babies, I should call them," said Reddy Squirrel. "I shouldn't like to have to rock them to sleep."

"Another thing," said Bunny Rabbit, "where would you get the rocks?" This tickled the animals so that Racky Coon nearly fell into the water.

All the animals were out of the plane except Reddy Squirrel; and, when asked why he didn't get out, he said: "I feel safer here. I'm not used to life on such an enormous scale. And besides, your new playmates are too big for me to play with."

"Say, Mr. Walrus," said Reddy Fox, "will you pardon me if I ask how much you weigh?"

"Not at all," said Mr. Walrus. "I weigh just over 2000 pounds, but there are walruses larger than I am."

"There is one thing I'd like to know," said Buster, "you seem to hear pretty well, but I don't see any ears."

"No," said Mr. Walrus, "our ears don't show much, but we have them just the same. The opening is deep in one of the deep folds of our skin."

The Animal Aviators were more than interested in these strange animals; but they decided to take to the air again, and soon the great walruses were just tiny specks in the distance.

They were sailing along quietly, when Buster Bear let out a cry as he looked down into the water. A great stream of water or vapor came up, almost to the plane; and then the ocean opened and a great shape came up out of the depths. "Goodness!" said Buster. "What's broken loose? I'm getting used to strange sights, but this beats all."

They had passed over this tremendous shape, but Buster came back in a great circle. He had no intention of getting too close to this unknown.

"What is it?" said Buster to Reddy Fox. "You are supposed to know all the answers."

"Let me see! Let me see! Why, that's a whale, the Right Whale."

"I'm glad it is not the wrong whale," said Reddy Squirrel.

"That whale is neither right nor wrong," said Reddy Fox. "That is the Right or Greenland Whale. That is its name."

"Well," said Reddy Squirrel, "I've made a mistake, but I'm not going to blubber about it."

"You two seem to be having a whale of a time," said Buster.

As they circled round this monster of the deep, Racky Coon said: "I never dreamed anything could grow so large."

"They sure are large," said Reddy Fox. "Some whales grow to be over 50 feet long and weigh over 100 times as much as those walruses that we have just seen."

"What does this big fish live on?" said Buster.

"I can tell you what food a whale lives on, but it is no fish," replied Reddy. "It is a mammal. And as for food, it lives on small fish. Those 'fountains' are merely the warm air being expelled from the whale's lungs. The warm air meets the cold air and becomes vapor."

After watching the whale a little longer, they turned the plane toward Iceland again.

The animals all began to say they were hungry. They had been unable to add to their food supplies since before their North Pole flight. They had only one or two boxes that they had not opened. "Well, animals," said Reddy Fox, "we have one big cheese left. How would you like some cheese sandwiches?" The animals all said they would.

"Say, Reddy Squirrel, you have sharp biting teeth, just cut the heavy cord that holds the cover on and I'll fix up a lunch," said Reddy Fox.

Reddy Squirrel went aft, cut the cord, and lifted the cover. As he did this, he let out a yell that brought the other animals right about face with a jump.

Flight is interrupted as stowaway pops out of cheese box

When asked whether he had been in the box all during the trip, Willie Whitefoot replied that his answer was "gnaw."

A Stowaway Mouse Is Found

As the cover to the big cheese box tumbled off, Reddy Squirrel was so startled that he jumped onto the elevator wings of the plane. Up came a little mouse into view, and waved to the other animals. He was so fat he could hardly stand on the edges of the cheese box. "You'll excuse me, animals, but I wanted to take this trip, and I felt you would not take me, as I'm a stranger to you. I am Willie Whitefoot, and I lived some way from Animal Town. There was such a crowd the day you started off, and, I peeked into this box before you tied it up; and as the cheese only half filled it, I hopped in and pulled on the cover. I'm sorry I ate all your cheese, but it was oh, so good."

"Say," said Reddy Squirrel, "you haven't been in that cheese box all the time, for in the back part is a big mouse hole."

"Why," said the little mouse, "do you suppose I'd stay there in that dark box all during the trip? My answer is 'gnaw.' When you animals were away from the plane I had a wonderful time and even when you were sailing along, I would peek out."

The other animals were speechless at first. Then Reddy Fox said, "We really should toss you overboard."

"Oh, you don't scare me a bit. I know you animals are too kindhearted; and before the trip is over I may be able to help you for this kindness."

While the animals tried to appear stern, they really had taken a great fancy to the little mouse.

Just then Buster Bear shouted: "Land ahead! I suppose this is Iceland, as it is only 250 miles from Greenland."

"Yes," said Reddy Fox, "this is Iceland."

They found the shores to be similar to Greenland's—quite high in spots. They were now over land, and how the animals peered with interested eyes down on this strange land! They sailed low to see as much as possible.

"I see a geyser and there is another over there," said Racky.

"Why this looks like the Yellowstone Park—and there are hot springs here also," said Reddy Fox.

"Oh!" shouted Racky Coon, "There is a caribou, same as we saw in Alaska."

Reddy Fox said, "You're a good one, Racky, when we were in Alaska, you called caribou, reindeer; now these are reindeer and you call them caribou."

"There is one of your relatives, Reddy Fox," said Bunny Rabbit. The animals looked as he pointed, and there was a beautiful white fox.

The plane was brought down and the animals approached the fox. Reddy Fox said, "Don't be afraid of us. We are just Animal Town folks on a good will trip around the world, visiting all our relatives."

The white fox turned his head slightly and looked at them with one eye. He decided that he had nothing to fear. Snowy White Fox, for this he said was his name, said, "I'll have to get up a party and introduce you to some of our animals." And before long the visitors were surrounded by all kinds of animals curious to see these strange visitors from foreign shores. They easily became acquainted and had a fine time playing games and having a contest of outdoor sports.

The time to leave came all too quickly, so saying 'good-by' to their newfound friends, the aviators once more headed out over the ocean; this time for the British Isles.

The Larry O'Toole Foxes entertain the Aviators in Ireland

Mr. Fox was a great fiddler, and Mrs. Fox
couldn't be beat at an Irish jig.

Aviators Land in Ireland

"I see land," shouted Reddy Fox, and all the other Animal Aviators could see through the fog the dim shape of land ahead.

"Looks as if they were building a bridge or something," said Racky Coon.

"That's no bridge," said Reddy Fox. "I don't blame you; it does look strange, but I've seen pictures of it. What we are now looking at is the Giant's Causeway, about the most northern part of Ireland."

"Well," said Reddy Squirrel, "I don't see any giants around."

"Now, Reddy Squirrel, get this," said Reddy Fox, "the Giant's Causeway is only a name given to this large rock formation. Somebody many years ago thought it looked as if giants had built it."

As they sailed along, each animal saw something the others didn't, and they were all talking and paw pointing at the same time. Presently, a large city came into view on the coast, with great buildings and lots of ships.

"This, according to my map," said Reddy Fox, "is Belfast, a great city, and where they manufacture lots of famous Irish linen."

Soon they were over a large lake.

"Wonder what the name of this lake is," said Buster Bear.

"They don't call this a lake," spoke up Reddy Fox. "All lakes are called loughs here in Ireland; and this is Lough Neagh, the largest in Ireland."

"A silly name, I call it," said Bunny Rabbit. "I thought a lake was a lake anywhere."

They passed over many villages, then another large city showed up.

"This is Dublin," said Reddy Fox. "The capital of Ireland."

"There seem to be a lot of bogs in this country," said Buster Bear.

"There surely are," said Reddy Fox. "My book tells me that one ninth of Ireland is composed of bogs. They cut up the earth in these bogs into small pieces, and burn it for heat and cooking. This is called peat."

"For the love of Pete, or the love of Mike," said Buster Bear, "this must be where these sayings came from."

"Say," said Bunny Rabbit, "I thought we came over here to visit animals and to study and not to look at cities."

"Well?" said Buster Bear. "I was just waiting till you stopped talking, to tell you there are some of Reddy Fox's relatives watching us from that little hill. Shall I land here?"

"Sure!" shouted all the aviators. And down they came like a bird. The Irish foxes were peeking from behind some stones, seemingly not much frightened.

"Hi! Hi!" shouted Reddy Fox. "We're friendly animals come to visit you from Animal Town."

The Foxes came up, saying, "Top of the mornin' to you, strangers! We've seen airplanes go over, but this is the first one that ever landed here."

They shook paws all around, and the Irish fox said, "I'm Larry O'Toole Fox. This is me wife, Biddy; and me two children, Skippy and Jumpy."

"Come into me home," and Mr. Fox showed it with pride. It was a fine cave, fitted up with bunks and rustic furniture that he had built himself.

"Don't you ever get lonesome?" asked Buster Bear.

"Oh no," said Mr. Fox. "The hounds give us lots of excitement. We lead them a merry chase once in a while, and men on horseback seem to be chasing the hounds."

"Say," piped up Reddy Squirrel from his perch in a small tree, "can hounds climb?"

"No," said Mr. Fox. "Not up where you are."

"Thanks," said Reddy Squirrel. "I can now enjoy myself."

"Well," said Mr. Fox, "it's great exercise; it keeps us limber. Come, me dear Biddy, give us a little Irish jig and I'll play for you on me little fiddle."

The aviators loved to hear Mr. Larry O'Toole Fox talk, it sounded so musical.

He went into his cave home and brought out his old fiddle. The way he played and the way Biddy danced the jigs and reels showed they were limber.

Buster Bear said he'd rather not be so limber if he had to be chased by hounds every few days.

The Animal Aviators enjoyed the little show the O'Toole Foxes put on for them. But soon they had to say 'good-by', and so they got into their plane once more.

And now our animal friends are off to even greater adventures. Soon they will be meeting more animal cousins and seeing other distant lands. Although they can never be sure exactly where their travels will lead them, now that they have crossed the Atlantic Ocean, all of Europe, Asia, Australia and Africa are theirs to explore.

If all goes well, the Animal Aviators expect their next landing to be in England. There they hope to meet deer, otter and many other animals as they learn more of the world beyond Animal Town.

Look for continued Animal Town adventures in Book II. Follow Buster Bear, Reddy Fox, Racky Coon, Reddy Squirrel, and now Willie Whitefoot as they meet other animal relatives and continue to spread their message of peace and good will on their adventure around the world.

Some words and their meanings
(A Glossary)

Adventure — Something exciting or new. A trip or journey which may lead to unknown risks or danger.

Aviator — Somebody who flies an airplane.

Balsam Fir — A tree that is always green. It is often used as a Christmas tree. You can find an oily, sweet-smelling sap in its bark, called balsam.

Banner — A colorful sign usually painted on cloth.

Beaver — A furry animal with a broad flat tail. Beavers can cut down trees with their sharp teeth. They are also very good at building dams and lodges (houses) in the water.

Bison — A large, shaggy animal. It has a large head and neck, short horns, and humped shoulders; buffalo.

Bog — Wet spongy ground. It usually has lots of moss and peat growing on it (see "moss" and "peat").

Bunk — A bed; a sleeping place.

Canal — A narrow water way.

Canvas — A picture painted on a piece of cloth stretched on a frame

Cave — A natural underground opening. Caves can be very big—big enough for people or bears to live in.

Caribou — A large deer of northern North America, related to the reindeer.

Chart	A map used for navigating.
Cockpit	The space in a small airplane for pilot and passengers. In a large passenger plane, it is the space for the pilot and crew.
Compass	A small round instrument for finding directions. It uses a magnetic needle which turns so that it always points north and south.
Courageous	Not afraid of anything; brave. For instance, it took "courage" for the animal aviators to set off on their round-the-world adventure not knowing what dangers they might meet.
Dam	Anything that stops up water in a river. It helps save water during dry times. Beavers build very good dams.
Engine	The part which makes something like a car or airplane move; motor.
Exhibition	A public show.
Expedition	A trip or journey
Fiddle	A musical instrument; violin. It has 4 strings and is played with a bow.
Geyser	A spring that spouts heated water and steam. The water is heated deep underground by the earth's heat.
Glacier	A large mass of ice that moves slowly over land. It is usually from 300 to 10,000 feet thick.
Good Will	A genuine feeling of kindness and love. The purpose of the Good Will Tour is to spread kindness and love.
Grandeur	Large and beautiful; important.
Grouse	A bird that looks a little like a chicken. It has a plump body and strong feathered legs.

Grove	A small group of trees without underbrush.
Hot Springs	Springs with water above 98 F. They are heated naturally under the ground.
Ice Floe	A large flat floating sheet of ice; an iceberg.
Jackknife	A pocket knife. It can be snapped open and closed.
Jig	A lively, springy dance.
Landscape	A view of natural scenery.
Ledge	A narrow, flat surface that sticks out from a wall of rock.
Lichen	Plants which usually grow on rocks or tree bark. They have no roots.
Loon	A bird that swims and dives. It eats fish and looks a little like a large duck when sitting on the water. Great Northern Diver.
Meadow	A stretch of land covered with grass.
Moose	The largest member of the deer family. It lives in Canada and northern United States. Also known as elk.
Moss	Small, green plants. They grow close together on moist ground, tree trunks, or rocks.
Musk Ox	A large, shaggy, slow animal. It eats grass, lichen, and other small plants. It lives only in Greenland and the northern part of North America.
Northern Lights	Flashes of light in the sky seen only at night. They are best seen in the arctic. Aurora Borealis.

Peat   Soil made up of decayed plants. It is found in marshy or damp regions called bogs (see bog).

Plateau   A large flat piece of land. It is always higher than the surrounding land.

Pond   Water with land all around it. It is usually smaller than a lake.

Poplar Bark   The outside layers of a poplar tree. Poplar bark is a favorite food of beavers.

Propeller   Blades on the front of an airplane. As the blades whirl around, they move the plane forward.

Ptarmigan   A small bird. It looks like a grouse (see grouse) with completely feathered feet. These feathers help the ptarmigan move across the snow.

Rainbow   A semi-circle of colors in the sky. You can see it when the sun shines through raindrops or mist.

Reel   A lively Scotch-Highland dance.

Roots   The underground part of a plant. They absorb water and minerals that plants need to grow.

Silhouette   An outline drawing, usually filled in with black. The side-view of something, but just the outline.

Spruce   A cone-bearing evergreen tree. It has short, needle-shaped leaves.

Squall   A sudden gust of wind with rain, snow, or sleet.

Stout   Strong; hearty.

Stream   A river; brook. A stream may start with melting snow, glacier, or an overflowing lake.

Taxi   To move at a slow speed on the ground (as an airplane taxied along the runway).

Town Hall   A building used for government offices and meetings.

Valley   A low-lying piece of land. It is usually between hills or mountains.

Voyager   Somebody who travels on a long journey.

Walrus   A large sea animal. It is related to the seal. It has a pair of large tusks, tough skin, and flippers. During the winter and spring, walruses drift on large floating pieces of ice.

Whale   A very large animal that lives in the ocean. It is not a fish, but is a mammal.

Wilderness   An area where usually only wild animals live and no people.